NO FAIR SCIENCE FAIR

NANCY POYDAR

Holiday House / New York

Text and illustrations copyright © 2011 by Nancy Poydar
All Rights Reserved
HOLIDAY HOUSE is registered in the U.S. Patent and Trademark Office.
Printed and bound in October 2010 at Tien Wah Press, Johor Bahru, Johor, Malaysia.
The text typeface is Billy.
The art was created with gouache and pencil.
www.holidayhouse.com
First Edition
1 3 5 7 9 10 8 6 4 2

Library of Congress Cataloging-in-Publication Data
Poydar, Nancy.
No fair science fair / Nancy Poydar. — 1st ed.
p. cm.
Summary: As the judging of his class's science fair approaches, Otis has trouble even thinking of an idea but once he has built a bird
feeder he is determined to make some good observations, no matter how long it takes.
ISBN 978-0-8234-2269-2 (hardcover)
[1. Persistence—Fiction. 2. Bird feeders—Fiction. 3. Science fairs—Fiction. 4. Schools—Fiction.] I. Title.
PZ7.P8846No 2011
[E]—dc22
2010023224

For the stick-to-it kids,
Billy and Felix

Mr. Zee's class was having a science fair. Otis had tried lots of project ideas.

"Remember, the judges will be here next Friday," chirped Mr. Zee.

"Next Friday!" Otis gulped.

"Don't forget, scientists are observers,"
continued Mr. Zee. "I spy with my little eye,"
he said, "something blue."

"A blue jay!" Otis pointed out the window.

Then Otis looked around the room. Rosie was looking at hair under a magnifying glass. Millie was seeing which popcorn popped the best. Jack was observing how much his plants had grown in the sun.

"All the good projects are taken," said Otis. "It's not fair; there's nothing left to observe."

"But when you said *blue jay*," said Mr. Zee, "I thought with my little brain—"

"Birds!" said Otis. "Cardinals, nuthatches, goldfinches . . ."

"It's hard to observe birds," warned Millie. "Birds fly away."

But Otis liked birds. He even knew some of their names. He had seen a bird project in a book.

On Monday, Otis brought an empty milk carton, birdseed, and a twig to school. He got out scissors, paint, and string.

"That doesn't look scientific," said Max. "My volcano is scientific."

"It's going to be a bird feeder," said Otis.

Millie came by. "I smell with my little nose . . . a milk carton."

"I washed it. It doesn't smell," said Otis. "It's a bird feeder."

"Birds don't drink milk," said Millie.

"I'm painting it," said Otis. "Then I'll fill it with seed."

Mr. Zee said, "You'll have to wait until tomorrow. Wet paint is sticky."

"I'm observing hair," said Rosie. *Snip.* "I don't have to wait."

On Tuesday, Otis filled his bird feeder with sunflower seeds. Mr. Zee let him hang it outside.

"Birds are too timid to come to a school feeder," said Jack.

But Otis stared out the window. He didn't want to miss a single chickadee at his feeder.

At the end of the day, Jack said, "Bad luck?"

"Tomorrow," said Otis. He wrote *Zero birds at my feeder* in his science fair notebook.

On Wednesday, Otis observed birdseed on the ground. "Look. I think that seed spilled while they were eating," he said.

"I spy with my little eye," said Jack, ". . . something furry."

"No fair. A squirrel." Otis sighed and wrote in his notebook.

"I see you're sticking with it," said Mr. Zee.

On Thursday, they worked on project posters. "Good projects start with a question," said Mr. Zee.

What does your hair look like? wrote Rosie.

What birds come to my bird feeder? wrote Otis. He drew a goldfinch. Then he looked up. "My feeder's jiggling! The birds must have been on it!"

"It's the wind," said Millie.

"No," said Otis. "Watch!"

But nobody observed birds at Otis's feeder, not even Otis.

Mr. Zee announced, "The judges will be in our room in the morning."

"No fair," muttered Otis.

That night Otis thought, *Wouldn't it be amazing to see birds at my feeder in the morning, on Science Fair Day? The judges would see them too.* He hoped so hard, he had bird dreams all night. *Goldfinches, cardinals, chickadees . . .*

On Friday morning, Otis's classroom *was* amazing. Max's volcano was about to erupt.

Otis checked his feeder. "Look! The birds almost finished the seeds!" But everyone was too busy to look at Otis's bird feeder.

Then Rosie whispered, "I spy with my little eye . . ."

"The judges!" whispered Millie.

23

When the judges got to Otis, the tall one asked, "Did you make that bird feeder?"

"Yes," said Otis, "but I'm still waiting for birds."

"Are you writing down what you observe?" asked the short judge.

"Yes," said Otis, "but I'm still watching for birds." The judges studied everything and moved on.

"Bad luck?" said Millie.

"No luck," said Otis, and he stared out the window.

Finally, it was time for prizes. "We can see you've all worked hard," began the tall judge. One by one she awarded prizes.

"Why are you still staring at that feeder?" said Rosie. "The judges already saw your project."

"For next year's science fair," said Otis. Then he heard his name.

"To Otis for his project—"What Birds Come to My Bird Feeder?"—we award the Stick-with-It Prize!"

"But I'm not done with it," said Otis.

"But you'll be sticking with it," said Mr. Zee.

"I spy with my little eye . . . ," cried Millie.

"Birds," said Otis, "at my feeder! A goldfinch. A chickadee. They need more seed."

"You're so lucky," said Jack.

"Stick-to-it-iveness isn't luck," said Mr. Zee.

What science project ideas can you observe in Mr. Zee's classroom?